SCOOBY-DOO!

AND THE

GHOSTLY GORILLA

Written by
James Gelsey

WORLDWIDE PUBLISHING

A
LITTLE APPLE
PAPERBACK

SCHOLASTIC INC.

New York Toronto London Auckland Sydney
Mexico City New Delhi Hong Kong Buenos Aires

To Michael C.

No part of this publication may be reproduced in whole or in part, or stored in a retrieval system, or transmitted in any form or by any means, electronic, mechanical, photocopying, recording, or otherwise, without written permission of the publisher. For information regarding permission, write to Scholastic Inc., Attention: Permissions Department, 555 Broadway, New York, NY 10012.

ISBN 0-439-28485-6

Designed by Carisa Swenson

12 11 10 9 8 7 6 5   2 3 4 5 6 7/0
Special thanks to Duendes del Sur for cover and interior illustrations.
Printed in the U.S.A.
First Scholastic printing, January 2002

Chapter 1

Fred sat behind the wheel of the Mystery Machine, guiding the van down the highway. Suddenly, a loud crash came from the back of the van.

"What's going on back there?" Fred called back.

"Like, everything's under control, Fred," Shaggy replied. "Scoob and I are just looking through our emergency provisions to make sure we have everything we need." Shaggy held a huge duffel bag upside down, shaking

1

the last of its contents onto the floor of the van. He and Scooby were surrounded by snacks, treats, and other edible goodies.

"Are you sure you packed them, Scoob?" Shaggy asked.

"Ri rink ro," Scooby replied.

Shaggy rummaged through the pile of food. Out of the corner of his eye, Shaggy noticed Scooby pick up a bag of Yummie Crunchies.

"Oh, no, you don't, Scooby, old pal," Shaggy said, grabbing the bag of snacks.

"Those are for emergencies only. Now, help me put this stuff back in the bag."

After they finished cleaning up, Shaggy poked his head up front.

"Hey, Daphne, did you remember to bring the blueberry muffins?" he inquired very casually. "Scooby seems to have forgotten them."

"Blueberry muffins?" Daphne exclaimed. "Why on earth would I bring blueberry muffins?"

"For the preserves," Shaggy explained. "Like, why else?"

"Shaggy, you're making less sense than usual," Velma called back. "What are you talking about?"

"I'm talking about spreading the preserves on the blueberry muffins," Shaggy stated. He demonstrated by pretending to spread imaginary preserves on an imaginary muffin. Then Scooby grabbed the imaginary muffin and pretended to swallow it.

"Mmmm," Scooby sighed, rubbing his stomach. "Rueberry muffin."

"I'm sorry, Shaggy, but we still don't get it," Fred added.

"Didn't you tell me and Scoob that we were going to get pumpernickel preserves today?" Shaggy asked.

Fred, Daphne, and Velma looked at one another and laughed.

"What's so funny?" asked Shaggy.

"You are," Daphne replied. "Shaggy, we're not going to get pumpernickel preserves today."

"Why not?" Shaggy said.

"First of all, there's no such thing," Velma said. "And second of all, we're going to a jungle nature center run by Dr. Abner Pumpernickel, the famous anthropologist. It's called the Pumpernickel Preserve."

"You mean the Pumpernickel Preserve

doesn't have pumpernickel or preserves?" Shaggy asked in astonishment.

"Nope," Velma answered.

"Are there, like, any spreadable toppings there?" Shaggy continued.

"I'm afraid not, Shaggy," Daphne said.

"Man, that's the worst news I've heard all day." Shaggy sighed. "So why are we going if they don't have anything sweet to eat?"

"We're going because Professor Pumpernickel is an old friend of my family's," Velma explained. "He invited us to check out his latest discovery."

"What is it this time, Velma?" Fred asked.

"On his last trip to Africa, he uncovered a lost civilization that worshiped gorillas," said

Velma. "He's re-created part of their village in the jungle preserve. And he told me he's got a surprise, too. Something very rare that he found in Africa and brought back here."

"Sounds a little creepy to me," Shaggy said.

"Well, it sounds groovy to me," Daphne said. "I can't wait to get there."

"You won't have to," Fred said. "We're here."

Fred stopped the Mystery Machine in front of a tall metal fence. Coils of barbed wire topped the fence as far as the eye could see.

"Well, whatever he's got here, it looks like Professor Pumpernickel wants to make sure it doesn't get out," Fred guessed.

"And make sure that anyone who's not supposed to doesn't get in," Velma added.

"It looks like that includes us," Shaggy said. "Oh, well, what do you say we go grab something to eat? Like some blueberry muffins."

But before Fred could answer, they heard a clanking sound. A gate in the tall metal fence slowly opened, revealing a long driveway into the jungle.

"Well, gang, here we go!" Fred said, putting the van into gear. "Time for a jungle adventure!"

Chapter 2

The Mystery Machine followed the road deep into the heart of the Pumpernickel Preserve. Tall, exotic trees and other greenery grew alongside the road, creating a natural canopy. Suddenly, Fred slammed on the brakes, sending Shaggy and Scooby tumbling into Daphne's and Velma's laps.

"Like, what's the big idea, Fred?" complained Shaggy.

"That!" Fred exclaimed, pointing to a furry white creature on the road in front of them.

"It looks like a gorilla," Velma said.

The gorilla stood up on its back legs and thumped its chest, letting out a loud roar.

"You mean an *angry* gorilla," Fred said.

"Or a c-c-creepy gorilla," Shaggy called out from under the seat.

The gorilla howled at the van. Then it turned and ran into the jungle.

"Remind me to ask Professor Pumpernickel about that," Velma said.

"Don't worry, I don't think any of us would forget that thing," Daphne replied.

Fred took his foot off the brake and the Mystery Machine continued on its way. The road ended next to a small hut with a thatched roof. A short man wearing a khaki vest and shorts waved to the van. His fluffy gray mustache curled at the ends, and his round eyeglasses shimmered in the sunlight.

Fred parked the van and the gang jumped out.

"Hi, Professor Pumpernickel!" Velma called as she ran over to him. He kissed Velma on the cheek and smiled at the rest of the gang. "Wonderful to see you again, Velma," Professor Pumpernickel said. "And who are these fine young people?"

"These are my friends," Velma said. "This is Fred, Daphne, Shaggy, and Scooby-Doo."

"Welcome, everyone, to my little slice of heaven," Professor Pumpernickel said grandly. "Now, before we head into the jungle, I want to show you my surprise, Velma."

"Is it some rare artifact you uncovered in Africa?" Velma asked eagerly.

"In a manner of speaking," Professor Pumpernickel said with a smile. Then he gave two short whistles, followed by a series of three grunts. Everyone heard a rustling sound come from the bushes behind the hut. A moment later, a gorilla slowly stepped out from behind a tree. It walked up behind Professor Pumpernickel, who did not seem to know it was there.

"Rikes!" Scooby barked, jumping into Shaggy's arms. "Rorilla!"

Before anyone could do anything, the gorilla jumped onto the professor's back.

"That gorilla's attacking the professor!" Shaggy exclaimed.

"If I didn't know better, I'd say he's tickling the professor," Fred stated.

"You're half right, Fred. This gorilla is tickling me," Professor Pumpernickel said between laughs. "But it's a she, not a he. Come on down, Dot."

The gorilla climbed off the professor's back and sat on the ground next to him.

"Everyone, this is Dot," Professor Pumpernickel said. "She was my rare find in Africa. She's the smartest gorilla I've ever encountered."

"If she's so smart, how come she doesn't listen?" asked a woman coming out of the jungle. She was dressed like the professor, in safari khakis. "I was getting her ready for lunch when all of a sudden she just up and ran." The woman turned to Dot and started scolding her.

"I'm sorry, Carolina, it was my fault," the professor apologized. "I wanted to introduce Dot to my friends. Please don't blame her."

Carolina whipped around. "You know, Professor, I was willing to go from being your research assistant to taking care of your pet gorilla because you said I'd have complete control over Dot," she complained. "That was two months ago, and you still haven't stopped interfering!"

"You're right, Carolina, but I can't help it," Professor Pumpernickel confessed. "When it comes to Dot, I guess I'm just a pushover."

"I can't work like this, Professor," Carolina warned. "If something like this happens again, I'm leaving." Carolina looked at her wristwatch. "Come on, Dot," she said sweetly. "It's almost time for your grooming. Let's go, baby." Carolina reached out her hand, and Dot grabbed it. The two of them walked back through the trees and disappeared into the jungle.

"What a sweet gorilla," Daphne said.

"That reminds me," Velma began. "Professor, on our way in, a huge white gorilla ran across the road and roared at us. Is that another of your rare finds from Africa?"

"A huge white gorilla, you say?" asked the professor. "Dot's the only gorilla around here that I know of. Now, what do you say we head on into the jungle? I've got so much to show you.

Chapter 3

rofessor Pumpernickel led the gang down
a narrow path. The deeper into the jungle
they walked, the louder the sounds of nature
became. Exotic birds sang and rustled in the
tree branches. The sweet fragrance of beauti-
ful flowers wafted through the air.

"This is an incredible place, Professor!"
Daphne exclaimed.

"Why, thank you, Daphne," Professor
Pumpernickel replied. "But you haven't
seen everything yet. Take a look at that!"

15

Professor Pumpernickel pointed to a large gorilla standing in front of them.

"Zoinks! It's that ghostly gorilla!" Shaggy shouted. "Last one back to the Mystery Machine's a rotten egg!" He and Scooby turned to run, but Fred was blocking their way.

"All right, you two," he said. "Get ahold of yourselves. It's just a statue."

Shaggy and Scooby turned around and saw that the gorilla was really a wooden statue.

"I found these things all over the village that I discovered in Africa," Professor Pumpernickel explained. They were made by a tribe that worshiped gorillas. The tribesmen used primitive tools to carve the gorilla shapes out of whole tree trunks. There's a legend that one of the statues even contains the largest diamond in the world."

"Jinkies! That statue must have been very hard to move here," Velma remarked.

"Actually, Velma, the tribesmen hollowed out the trunk first," Professor Pumpernickel said. "The statues are surprisingly light. Only about thirty pounds."

"If you ask me, they might as well be a thousand pounds," said a man emerging from the bushes. He was dressed in safari khakis like Professor Pumpernickel, but he had his name embroidered on the shirt pocket. The man scratched the back of his head with his right arm and scratched his right arm with his left arm.

"You're not supposed to move them, Mr. McDoone," the professor scolded.

"I wasn't trying to move one," Mr. McDoone replied. "I bumped into a banana tree by the village and got some sap on me. I'm allergic to anything bananalike, and I started itching like nobody's business. I scratched my back against one of the statues and it didn't even budge."

"Just try to be careful, please, Mr. Mc-Doone," pleaded Professor Pumpernickel. "I know that you paid for the preserve, and I'm very grateful, but I have to ask you to watch out for the artifacts. They're thousands of years old."

"Take it easy, Abner," Mr. McDoone said. "They've lasted this long, haven't they? A little back scratching won't hurt them. Besides,

you've got more important things to worry about. I think I saw a hole in the fence in the northeast corner. You'd better go check it out."

"A hole, you say? Yes, yes, I'd better go," Professor Pumpernickel said. "I'll catch up with you soon, Velma. Follow this path to the village."

Professor Pumpernickel disappeared into the jungle.

"So are you kids working with the professor or something?" asked Mr. McDoone.

"Not exactly," Velma replied. "But I've known him for years."

"I see," Mr. McDoone said. "Then I'm sure he's mentioned me. Marty McDoone. The 'money man.'"

Velma shook her head.

"That's all right, I'm not in it for the money," Mr. McDoone said. "Aw, who am I kidding? Of course I'm in it for the money. In fact, I spent just about all of mine to bankroll

Abner's expedition and bring all those artifacts back from Africa. I need to get a return on my investment, so I'm planning on turning this science fair project into a money-making proposition. All I need is a little more money, a few more animals, and voilà — instant zoo!"

"Does Professor Pumpernickel know about this?" asked Fred.

"Not yet," Mr. McDoone replied. "I'll break the news to him gently. Until then, I hope I can count on you to keep this our little secret." He stopped scratching long enough to look at his wristwatch. "Oh, dear, not much time left. I've got a few more statues to examine. Have a nice afternoon."

Marty McDoone turned and ran back into the jungle.

"Like, watch out for those banana trees!" Shaggy called after him.

Chapter 4

"Like, now what do we do?" asked Shaggy. "We're lost in the jungle."

"We're not lost, Shaggy," Velma said. "Professor Pumpernickel said we should follow the path to the village."

The gang walked around the big gorilla statue and continued along the path. They heard a rustling sound in the trees above them and heard someone yell, "WHOOOOAAAAA!" Then something fell onto the path in front of them with a thud.

"It's the ghostly gorilla!" Shaggy exclaimed.

"It's a man!" Daphne shouted. "Let's go see if he's okay."

The man stood up slowly. He was dressed in green camouflage clothes. He dusted himself off and then looked up into the trees.

"Guess I didn't have as good a grip on that vine as I thought," he muttered. Then he looked at the gang and saw the concern on their faces. "Sorry to scare you like that, folks."

"Are you all right?" asked Daphne.

"I'm fine, thanks," the man answered. "I just lost my grip, that's all."

"If you don't mind us asking, what were you doing up in that tree?" asked Velma.

"I've been living up in that

tree for" — the man answered as he looked at his wristwatch — "three, two, one. I've been living up in that tree for exactly three days, ten hours, and twenty-six minutes. I'm Rudy Biggler."

"That name sounds familiar," said Velma. "I remember reading about an animal rights activist named Rudy Biggler. He once strapped himself to a tree to stop a real estate developer from clearing a forest."

"Actually, I did it to save the rare striped butter owl that lived in the tree," the man explained.

"You're the same Rudy Biggler?" asked Daphne. "What are you doing in a nature preserve?"

"I'm here on a secret mission to figure out how to return the animals to their natural habitats," replied Rudy. "Especially the rare gorilla."

"You mean Dot?" asked Fred.

"That's right," Rudy continued. "No creature deserves to be taken thousands of miles away from its home. So I'm going to get that gorilla back to Africa if it's the last thing I do."

"Like, how are you going to do that?" asked Shaggy.

"I'm working on a two-part plan," Rudy said. "The first part is too complicated to explain right now. And the second part involves getting my hands on the money to do it."

The gang heard a whistling sound in the distance. Rudy Biggler whipped his head around in the direction of the whistle. He tilted his head and listened.

"Sounds like a rare billow-beaked whippoorwill," he said. "Once they start, there's no stopping that noise. They'll blow my cover for sure." Rudy turned back to the kids. "No

one knows I'm here, and you'll be doing en-
dangered animals everywhere a great service
if you keep it that way."

Before anyone could answer, Rudy
jumped up and grabbed a low-hanging
branch. He swung his legs up in the air and
disappeared into the dense foliage with a
quick flip. The gang heard the whistling
sound again, but this time it was louder.

"Sounds like that bird is getting closer,"
Fred said. "I wonder if we'll be able to see it."

"I think so," Velma said. "In fact, I think
it'll be hard to miss. Look."

Carolina walked through an opening in
the foliage, looking around and whistling.

"Yoo-hoo, Dot, honey," she called. "Time for lunch."

"Hey, that billow-beaked whippoorwill looks just like Dot's baby-sitter," Shaggy said.

"I'm not her baby-sitter," Carolina snapped. "In any event, have you seen her? She eats every five hours like clockwork and never misses a meal."

"Never misses a meal?" Fred said. "Sounds like someone we know."

"Please keep your eyes open for Dot," Carolina continued. "She likes to play tricks on people, so watch out. By the way, the professor's waiting for you at the village."

Carolina ignored the comment and continued on her way.

"Come on, Shaggy and Scooby," Daphne said. "Let's go find Professor Pumpernickel."

"Daphne, you've got to stop saying his name," Shaggy warned. "We're so hungry, Scooby and I are liable to eat him up."

Chapter 5

T he gang followed the path to a clearing where there was a row of five huts. In front of the huts stood a circle of six tall gorilla statues. Professor Pumpernickel was standing inside the circle. Seven or eight much smaller gorilla statues surrounded him.

"I don't know what Mr. McDoone was talking about," the professor said. "I couldn't find any hole in the fence. He must have been mistaken."

"Jinkies, Professor, what is all this?" asked Velma.

"This is a re-creation of what the village

looked like," explained the professor. "The tribespeople lived in huts just like those. They stored all of their handmade hunting and farming tools in one of them and used the rest for sleeping. Dot likes to sleep in the one on the end. When she's not here, she's usually under her favorite tree, eating."

"Speaking of eating . . ." Shaggy began.

Daphne and Velma shot him stern looks.

"What are all of these statues for?" asked Fred.

"This is where the tribespeople would keep their statues," Professor Pumpernickel continued. "According to their customs, they would summon a legendary white gorilla to save them from animal attacks, heavy rains, and things like that."

"How did they summon this white gorilla?" asked Velma. She was very interested in what the professor was saying.

"They chanted a special prayer carved

into the statues," the professor said. He picked up one of the small statues and showed it to Velma. She examined it, then handed it to Fred and Daphne. "I managed to translate their language into sounds we could pronounce," the professor continued. He handed Shaggy a little slip of paper with some writing on it.

"Hey, look, Scoob," Shaggy called. "It looks like something you'd find inside a gorilla fortune cookie." Shaggy looked at the words. "'*Rigg narl ronmoll chu,*'" he read.

"Not so loud," the professor warned. "Not that I believe in the gorilla legend, mind you.

But you never know. Would you like to see the inside of the huts?"

"Scoob and I would really like to see the inside of a restaurant," Shaggy suggested.

"I'm sure you must be hungry," Professor Pumpernickel said. "Why don't you grab a banana from those trees over there? They're very good. If you don't believe me, just ask Dot."

Shaggy and Scooby walked over to a large banana tree. A bunch of bright yellow bananas hung from a branch. Shaggy reached up to grab a banana. As he started pulling it, he heard a soft growling sound.

"Okay, Scooby, I know you're hungry, but tell your stomach to settle down," Shaggy said.

"Rat rasn't my romach," Scooby replied.

The growl got louder. Shaggy and Scooby slowly backed away from the banana tree.

"Uh, Fred? Velma? Daphne?" called Shaggy. "Like, could you come here, please?"

The three kids came out of the hut, followed by the professor.

"What is it now, Shaggy?" asked Velma. "Didn't you have any bananas?"

"No," Shaggy replied. "They growled at me."

"Bananas don't growl," Fred said.

"Bananas don't," Daphne said. "But gorillas do! Look!"

Just then, the ghostly white gorilla jumped out from behind the banana tree and roared at them.

"Zoinks!" Shaggy exclaimed.

"Jinkies!" shrieked Velma.

"Rikes!" barked Scooby.

Everyone ran inside one of the huts as the

gorilla approached the clearing. It knocked over two of the big statues, then looked at the bunch of little ones. One by one, it picked up each of the little statues and shook them. When it heard something rattle inside one, the gorilla clutched the statue close to itself. Before it ran off, the gorilla walked to the hut where everyone was hiding. It bent down, lifted up the side of the hut, and flipped the entire thing over.

"RRRRROOOOOOOOOOAAAAAAAAAR-

RRRRRRRR!" the gorilla howled. Then it turned and escaped into the jungle.

"Oh dear, oh my, oh dear, oh my," the professor said as he ran over to the altar. He examined all the little statues, shaking them.

"Oh, no!" he moaned. "That gorilla has the diamond."

"I thought you said it was just a myth," Velma said.

"That's what I tell everyone," Professor Pumpernickel answered sadly. "It's the only way to keep the treasure-seekers away. But there really is a diamond. And I guess there really is a mighty white gorilla, too."

"And that means there really is a mystery for us to solve," Fred said.

"Don't worry, Professor Pumpernickel," Velma assured him. "Mystery, Inc. is on the case!"

Chapter 6

"**Q**uick, let's follow the gorilla before it can get too far," Fred suggested.

The gang took off after the gorilla, trying to follow its path through the brush. A little way into the jungle, Scooby let out a howl.

"Rouch!" he cried, grabbing his tail.

"What's the matter, Scooby?" asked Shaggy.

"Rat ranch ratched ree," Scooby complained.

Daphne examined Scooby's tail. "There's

only a little scratch," she reported. "You'll be fine, Scooby."

"Hey, Scooby, it looks like you're going gray," Shaggy said. He bent down and picked up a tuft of whitish fur from under the branch that had scratched Scooby.

"That's not Scooby's fur," Velma said. She looked at it closely.

"Could it be the gorilla's fur?" asked Daphne.

"It's not gorilla fur, but I have a hunch it *is* the fur of the gorilla we're chasing," Velma said.

"Like, I don't get it," Shaggy said.

"Velma means that it's not real gorilla fur," Daphne explained. "Which means that our gorilla isn't a real gorilla."

"Gang, I think it's time to split up," Fred said. "Daphne, you come with me and see if we can find any more clues like this one."

"Shaggy, Scooby, and I will go back to the

village and see if we can find anything there," Velma said. "Let's meet back there as soon as we can."

"Great," Fred agreed. "Let's go, Daph."

He and Daphne continued into the jungle.

"All right, you two, let's head back to the village," Velma instructed. "And keep your eyes open along the way for possible clues."

Velma led Shaggy and Scooby back through the jungle to the village. "Professor Pumpernickel? Professor Pumpernickel!" she called. But no one answered.

"Maybe he went back to his office to make us lunch," Shaggy said.

"Or maybe he has more important things to do," Velma said. "Now, you two look around by the huts. I'm going to check out the statues and the area where the gorilla appeared."

Shaggy and Scooby slowly made their

way over to the row of huts. They saw the one that the gorilla had tipped over.

"All right, Scooby, let's start looking in these huts for clues," Shaggy said.

Scooby started heading through the hut's door. But Shaggy stopped him. "Hold on, Scoob," he interrupted. "Let's make this interesting. I'll give you my half of our emergency provisions if you can lift up one of these huts like that gorilla did."

"Hmmmmm," Scooby said, looking at the hut. "Rokay."

Scooby stood up on his hind legs. He spit into his front paws and rubbed them together. Then he slid his right paw under the side of the hut. He straightened out his tail, grabbed it with his left paw, and started pumping it up and down like a car jack. The hut slowly started lifting off the ground.

"Ree-hee-hee-hee-hee-hee," giggled Scooby.

"All right, pal, you win," Shaggy conceded.

Scooby kept pumping until he lifted the hut so high they could see something inside. It was Dot, and she was sleeping. "Ruh-roh," Scooby said.

"You'd better put it down gently, Scoob," Shaggy suggested. "We don't want to wake her up."

But Scooby lost his grip and the hut came crashing down. In a flash, Dot ran out the door, shrieking and jumping around. When she saw Scooby,

Dot ran over, grabbed him, and hugged him like a teddy bear.

"What's going on over here?" Velma asked, racing over to meet her friends.

"Uh, nothing really," Shaggy said. "Dot and Scooby are just hanging out, that's all. Did you find any clues?"

"All I found were a couple of banana peels that you and Scooby left behind," Velma said. "You know, you really need to clean up after yourselves."

"But we didn't have any bananas," Shaggy protested. "That ghoully gorilla jumped out of the trees before we could eat any."

"Well, if you didn't leave them, then who did?" wondered Velma.

"I don't know," Shaggy said. "Maybe it was Dot."

When she heard her name, Dot looked up and saw the banana peels. She let go of Scooby. She reached out and gently took them from Velma's hand, then stuffed them into her mouth.

"I don't think Dot left those banana peels," Velma reasoned. "But I have a hunch I know who did. I'm going to find Fred and Daphne and tell them about this." Velma turned and started walking back into the jungle.

"Like, wait for us, Velma!" Shaggy called. He and Scooby ran into the jungle after her.

Chapter 7

Shaggy and Scooby tried to follow Velma through the jungle, but they quickly lost sight of her.

"Man, this is just what I was afraid of," Shaggy moaned. "We'd better turn around and head back to the village."

Shaggy and Scooby turned to go. Each started walking off in a different direction.

"Hey, Scoob, where are you going?" asked Shaggy. "The village is this way."

"Ruh-uh," Scooby disagreed. "Ris ray." Scooby pointed in the direction he was going.

Shaggy looked in that direction — and saw the ghostly gorilla leap out of the bushes! "ZOINKS! It's the big white gorilla!" he cried. "Let's get out of here!"

Shaggy took off, with Scooby close behind him. The ghostly gorilla chased them under branches, around trees, and over rocks. The two friends kept fleeing, afraid to look back and see how close the ghostly gorilla was. After a while, Shaggy had to stop to catch his breath.

"Okay, Scoob," Shaggy panted. "I think we lost him." He looked around. "Come to think of it, I think we lost us, too. We'll never find our way out of here."

"Tell me about it," echoed

a familiar voice. Marty McDoone came out from under an enormous branch that was hanging low to the ground. "I still haven't figured out where I parked my car. Why are you two so out of breath?"

"That ghostly gorilla's been after us," answered Shaggy.

"You mean Dot?" asked Marty. "I wouldn't exactly call her ghostly."

"No, I mean that great big white gorilla. The one that stole the diamond and has been chasing us all around this place," Shaggy explained.

"Stole the diamond?" Marty repeated slowly. "A big white gorilla stole the diamond? Of all the luck! I've been wandering around this horrible jungle for hours and some dumb gorilla finds the diamond and steals it? I've gotta find that gorilla!"

Before Shaggy and Scooby could say anything else, Marty McDoone ran back into the jungle.

"If you ask me, Scoob, that guy is a few bananas short of a bunch," Shaggy said.

He and Scooby laughed.

"I'd know that laugh anywhere," a voice said. "Scooby-Doo! Where are you?"

"Hey, it's Daphne!" Shaggy exclaimed. "Like, we're not lost anymore! Over here, Daph!"

A moment later, Daphne, Velma, and Fred walked through the trees. Scooby ran up to Daphne and gave her a big hug and a kiss. Then he did the same to Velma and Fred.

"Okay, Scooby, we get it. You missed us," Fred said, laughing. "But where have you been? We've been looking everywhere for you."

"Man, you wouldn't believe it," Shaggy said. "First we got lost. Then that overgrown monkey chased us, so we got even more lost. Then that nutty Marty McDoone showed up. All this because we couldn't find our way back to the village." Shaggy shook his head.

"What do you mean?" asked Velma. "The village is just on the other side of that big branch."

"Shaggy, you and Scooby have been going in circles this whole time," Daphne explained.

A chirping sound suddenly filled the air.

"Hey, isn't that the something-beaked whipper-snapper bird?" Shaggy said.

"That's no bird," Velma said. "It's an alarm on a wrist-watch." The gang followed the sound back to the village. Fred found the watch on the ground next to the banana tree.

"I used to have a

45

watch just like this," Fred said. He stopped the beeping and then pushed one of the buttons on the side of the watch.

"That's interesting," he said. "The alarm is set to go off again in five hours."

"If this clue means what I think it means," Velma said, "I have a hunch our gorilla's time is up."

"Velma's right," Fred agreed. "Gang, let's set a trap."

Chapter 8

"Okay, gang, listen up," Fred said. "All we have to do is wait for that big white gorilla to come back into the village. Shaggy, you and I will hide behind one of the tall statues. Once the gorilla appears, Scooby will lure it over to us and we'll use one of the nets from the storage hut to capture it. That should hold it until Professor Pumpernickel gets back."

"Excuse me, Fred, but Scooby and I have some bad news," Shaggy said.

"What kind of bad news?" asked Daphne.

"We'd love to come to this little gorilla-catching party you're throwing," Shaggy said, "but we're having a party of our own this afternoon."

"What kind of party?" Fred asked.

"The kind where we hide in a tree and have nothing to do with catching a gorilla," Shaggy replied. "Come on, Scooby, we don't want to be late."

Shaggy and Scooby started walking away.

"Hold on there, you two," Daphne said. "We really need your help. Won't you help us, Scooby?"

"How about for all the bananas you can eat?" asked Velma.

"Ruh-uh," Scooby said.

"How about for a banana cream pie?" Daphne offered.

Scooby thought for a moment, then shook his head.

"How about for a banana cream pie with a Scooby Snack on top?" tried Velma.

Scooby's ears perked up. "Rokay!" he barked.

"I'll tell you what," Daphne said. "You can have the Scooby Snack now, and I'll bake the banana cream pie for you later." She tossed a Scooby Snack into the air. Scooby gobbled it down.

"Now that we've got that settled, let's get ready," Fred said. "Shaggy, you come with me to get the net. Scooby, you stay out here and wait for the gorilla."

"And Daphne and I will go get Professor Pumpernickel from his research station," Velma said.

"Like, good luck, Scoob," Shaggy called

as he followed Fred into the storage hut.

Scooby stood alone in the middle of the village. He whistled nervously, hoping that the ghostly gorilla wouldn't show up until after Fred and Shaggy came back. But suddenly, he heard a low growling sound from the bushes.

"Rikes!" Scooby said to himself, looking for somewhere to hide. There was no place. So he grabbed a couple of branches from the ground and held them in front of himself like a shield. Scooby tried to stand perfectly still and blend in with the trees. But he was so scared, the leaves on the branches kept rustling. Then something walked up behind him and started breathing so close that Scooby could smell the bananas on its breath.

"Ruh-roh!" Scooby barked. He put down the branch, turned around, and saw the big white gorilla standing there. "Raggy!" Scooby quickly handed the gorilla the branches, positioning them so they covered up almost all of it. Then he slowly tiptoed away.

The gorilla was momentarily confused. Then it threw down the branches, let out an enormous roar, and started running after Scooby. The huge white beast chased Scooby all over the village. They ran by the storage hut just as Fred and Shaggy were coming out with the net.

"Zoinks!" Shaggy exclaimed. Before Shaggy and Fred could move out of the way, the gorilla grabbed the net and ran around them three times, wrapping them up. "Man, now I know what a tortilla feels like," moaned Shaggy.

The gorilla chased Scooby around the tall statues. Scooby raced over to the trees by the edge of the village. Just as the gorilla reached out to grab his tail, something whisked Scooby up into the air. The ghostly gorilla tripped and fell forward. As it stood up, something hit it on the head. The gorilla looked down and saw that it was a banana. Then another banana hit the gorilla on the head. And another. And another. And another.

The gorilla looked up and saw Dot and

Scooby sitting in a tree. They were laughing and hurling banana after banana at the ghostly gorilla. The gorilla tried to run away, but there were so many bananas on the ground, it started slipping and sliding all over the place. The gorilla lost its balance and crashed into one of the tall gorilla statues. The statue toppled over, trapping the gorilla beneath a pile of mushy bananas.

Chapter 9

F red and Shaggy freed themselves from the net and ran over to the gorilla. Dot climbed down from the tree and helped Scooby get down, too.

Professor Pumpernickel burst through the foliage with Daphne and Velma behind him.

"My village!" he gasped in utter disbelief. "It's — it's — it's —"

"Ranana-ricious!" Scooby barked, licking some banana off his paw.

Then Professor Pumpnickel saw the big white gorilla on the ground.

"You caught it!" he exclaimed.

"And now would you like to see who stole your diamond?" Fred asked.

"And how!" replied the professor. He walked over to the big white gorilla and grabbed hold of its head. With a swift yank, he removed it. "Carolina? You're the ghostly gorilla?"

"Just as we suspected, Professor," Velma said.

"In a million years, I never would have guessed," said Professor Pumpernickel. "How did you know?"

"Well, sir, it wasn't easy at first," Fred said. "We found clues that made us believe it could have been any number of people."

"Or gorillas," Daphne added.

"Daphne's right," Velma said. "When we first saw the white gorilla on the road when we came in, we thought it was a real gorilla."

"But then we found the first clue," Fred

said. "A tuft of the gorilla's hair that came from a costume. That meant we weren't dealing with a gorilla at all, but with someone dressed up like a gorilla."

"So right there we guessed it could have been anyone with a reason to want the diamond, starting with Marty McDoone," Velma said.

"Mr. McDoone told us he wanted to turn the jungle preserve into a zoo," Daphne explained. "But that he didn't have enough money to do it yet."

"Then there's Rudy Biggler, the environmentalist," Velma said. "He's been hiding out here in your preserve trying to figure out a way to get enough money to return all of your animals to their natural habitats."

"You mean someone's been living here and I never knew it?" asked Professor Pumpernickel. "Amazing!"

"And then, of course, there's Carolina, who made it clear she was frustrated with having to take care of Dot," Fred added. "Any of them could have left that first clue."

"The banana peels we found over there told us the gorilla was probably snacking before it stole the diamond," Velma said. "And Marty McDoone is allergic to bananas. So that eliminated him as a suspect."

"That left Carolina and Rudy," Daphne said. "And the last clue."

Fred reached into his pocket and took out the watch.

"But anyone could wear a watch," Professor Pumpernickel.

"True, but not everyone would have its alarm set to go off every five hours," Velma said. "Unless, of course, they needed to be reminded to do something. Like feed a gorilla."

"Only Carolina would know when Dot wasn't going to be in the village," Daphne said. "That made it easier for her to come here disguised as the ghostly gorilla."

"But why would you steal from me, Carolina, after all I've done for you?" asked Professor Pumpernickel.

"All you did for me was turn me into a glorified gorilla nanny," Carolina complained. "I did it so I could sell the diamond and use the money to start an expedi-

tion of my own! I had this whole thing
planned out for weeks and was this close to
getting away with it all. Then that goofy dog
and his friends showed up and ruined everything!"

Before Carolina could say another word,
Dot walked over and stuffed a banana into
her mouth.

"Well, kids, I sure am grateful to you,"
Professor Pumpernickel said. "Especially
you, Scooby-Doo. How can I thank you?"

"I think Dot will take care of that for you, Professor," Velma said.

Dot took another banana and carefully peeled it. She gave the banana to Scooby and grabbed another banana for herself. She and Scooby each tossed their food into the air and gobbled them down together.

"Scooby-Dooby-Doo!" barked Scooby.

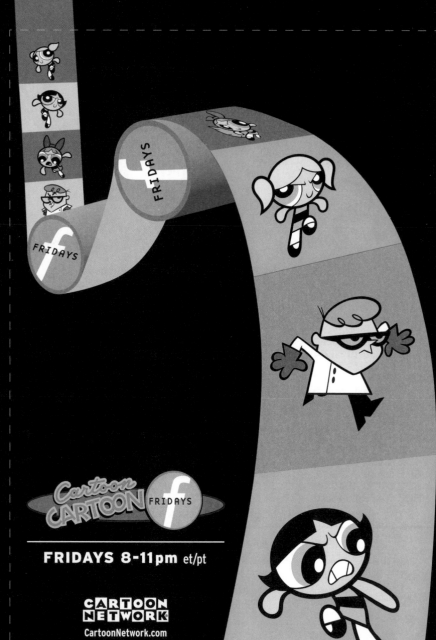

Cartoon CARTOON FRIDAYS f

FRIDAYS 8-11pm et/pt

CARTOON NETWORK
CartoonNetwork.com